This Book Belongs To:

_____

The Sailing Snailor

A RHYMING MERMAID TALE

Written & Illustrated by K. Michelle Edge

This book is dedicated to my niece
Maddie Rae Edge
Happy 2nd Birthday sweet girl!

The Sailing Snailor
A Rhyming Mermaid Tale
www.michelle-edge.com * kmichelleedge@gmail.com
South Jordan, Utah

Paperback ISBN: 978-1-63944-317-8

There once was a **SNAILOR** that sailed the seven **SEAS**.
He was the captain of his ship and he loved the ocean **BREEZE**.

He had a crack in his shell and a star on his SIDE.
He was the snailiest bug around, and a handsome
little GUY.

He loved the rocky waters; they filled his heart with PRIDE.
But, he had one true love and she lived below the TIDE.

She was a beautiful princess mersnail that roamed the ocean BLUE. She loved the sailing SNAILOR that she gave her whole heart TO.

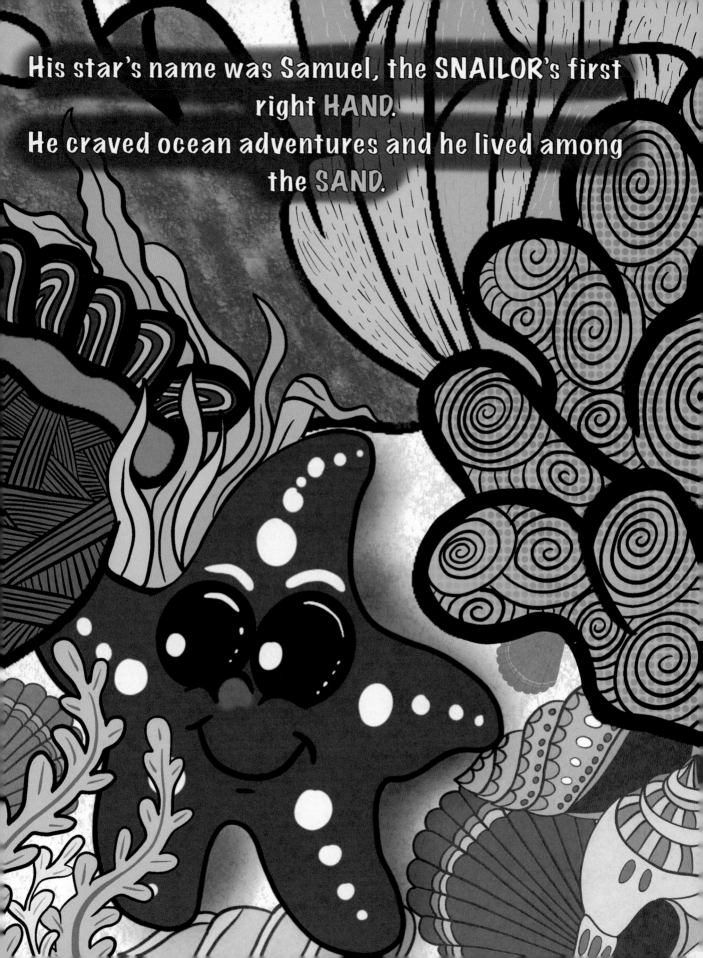

His star's name was Samuel, the SNAILOR's first right HAND.
He craved ocean adventures and he lived among the SAND.

The SNAILOR welcomed every storm and triumphed every WAVE.
He was the toughest snail around.... strong, courageous and BRAVE.

She lived in a palace of treasures, made of coral and ROCK.
She wore pearls in her crown and seashells in her TOP.

The **SNAILOR** searched for the treasure as he was on his **WAY**, and then he heard a scream just beyond the **BAY**.

An octopus grabbed his love, living deep BELOW.
"I must jump in and save her! Yo-HO-HO-HO!"

Samuel, the star, hung on tight as the **SNAILOR** dove down **DEEP**.
The swim was long and tiring, since he didn't have two **FEET**.

"Release my love, you giant monster! She's caused no harm to YOU!
I'll protect the princess with my life! To her my heart reigns TRUE."

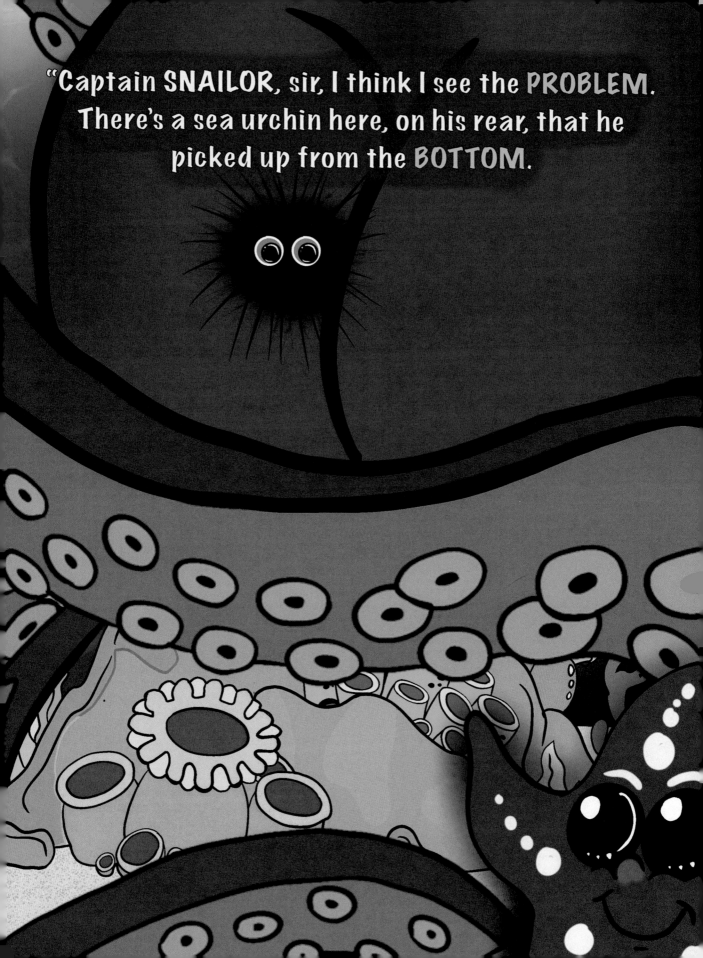

"Captain SNAILOR, sir, I think I see the PROBLEM. There's a sea urchin here, on his rear, that he picked up from the BOTTOM.

"I know that has to hurt because urchins are quite so SPINY.
I'll go down there to get it, sir, and pull it off his HINEY.

"Keep the princess calm and the angry giant STILL. Your love life seems so wild to me. You must just love the THRILL."

Sam removed the urchin and the giant let out a ROAR.
"Sorry about that sting, big guy. You may be a wee bit SORE."

The gentle giant released his love and she
swam to the **SNAILOR**'s **SIDE**.
"Thank goodness that you came for me!
Thank goodness I'm **ALIVE**!"

The giant monster swam away, and all were safe and WARM.
He's had a rough, tough sea life day. He meant no one such HARM.

"I was scared and helpless and so alone. I'm glad you heard my SCREAMS. You're such a brave, courageous snail, the SNAILOR of my DREAMS."

When they surfaced to the top, the crew helped them to CLIMB.
The sun was setting slowly; they were just in TIME.

They sailed into the horizon with two hearts full of LAUGHTER.
The SNAILOR and his princess lived happily ever AFTER.

About the Author/Illustrator

K. Michelle Edge, self-proclaimed "feral child", spent her childhood surrounded by nature and wilderness on her family's fish farm in Soperton, Georgia, which is still in operation today. Her younger days consisted of swimming in the creek, hunting, fishing, and playing with the wild and domesticated animals on the property.

Her love for the environment and being outside led her to many adventures, including falconry, rockhounding, sea turtle conservation, coral reef restoration, and wildlife rehabilitation. Ms. Edge has a degree in Natural Resources from Oregon State University, graduating Cum Laude as a first generation college student. To this day, she still loves to fish and hunt and is an avid SCUBA diver. She also prefers to be barefoot most of the time and finds that "city living" can be a challenge. She currently resides outside of Salt Lake City, UT, but always honors her true Southern upbringing.

OTHER TITLES BY THE CREATOR

FOLLOW US ON SOCIAL MEDIA

@kmichelleedge

<u>*Why is rhyming important?*</u>

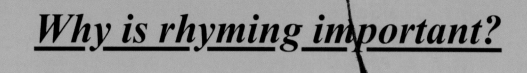

1. Rhyming teaches children how language works. It helps them notice and work with the sounds within words.

2. Rhymes help children experience the rhythm of language. As they recite nursery rhymes, they learn to speak with animated voices. Someday, they'll read with expression too!

3. When children are familiar with a nursery rhyme or rhyming book, they learn to anticipate the rhyming word. This prepares them to make predictions when they read, another important reading skill.

Name:_____ Date:_____

The Sailing Snailor Wordsearch
Find each word within the square and circle or highlight it individually.

```
L R D F Z P C O C X Z D F W T S W I M
A K Z K F X Y U S M F E I U L L A U D T
R Y G E J M Q H N V E A H R D K L B Z A
O M E R M A I D   R E L A C B W R N V I
C O O G S P I E F W S E W H Q A X S R L
S B T S H E L L S   P E P I W X B G R R
U M A W W D Y K K Z C   A N P   H D G T
B N M E U E Z C A K E X Z   E S Y D F M
D W D A B O A T F U E J X L E K U F O Q
S V A R T R O B C E M Y T S E V A W N X
J G H T C C E S Y W R S H H N M N G H Q
G Q Q S E E E N K L A Q S S U Z L P M I
G A R A F R D N R C L Z D M I N W O G V
K P N S J L E G S Z U R Z P F C S V T
K L B C I W T G J E O G S Q K T M U V E
  L I A N S E F Z L W C K D O M Y U X L
Q O A W N Z C O C B I O I P F U A S R Q
Z K O O U B F N P B D A U S D V L T F Z
V O M D S T Q S M U V S S L B G N A R F
G M X T L U I R U B   N H K B I E R E S
```

BOAT	BUBBLES	CASTLE
CLOUDS	CORAL	CRACK
FISH	LOVE	MERMAID
MONSTER	OCEAN	OCTOPUS
PEARLS	REEF	RESCUE
SAIL	SAND	SEA
SHELLS	SHIP	SNAIL
STAR	SUN	SWIM
TAIL	URCHIN	WATER
WAVES		

Answers

The Sailing Snailor Word Search

Find each word within the square and circle

L	R	D	F	Z	P	C	O	C	X		
A	K	Z	K	F	X	Y	U				
R	Y	G	E	J	M	Q	H				
O	M	E	R	M	A						
C	O	O	G	S	P						
S	B	T									
U	M	A	W	W	D	Y					
B	N	M	E	E	Z	C					
D	W		A								
S	V					B					
J	G										
G	Q					N	K				
G	A	R				N	R	C			
K	P	N				E					
K	L	B	C			G	J				
		I	A			F	Z				
Q	O	A	W	N	Z	C	O	C			
Z	K	O	O		B	F	N	P			
V	O	M	D		T	Q	S	M			
G	M	X	T	L	U	I	R	U			

BOAT
CLOUDS
FISH
MONSTER
PEARLS
SAIL
SHELLS
STAR
TAIL
WAVES

BUBBLES
CORAL
LOVE
OCEAN
REEF
SAND
SHIP
SUN
URCHIN

CRAB
MERMAID
OCTOPUS
RESCUE
SEA
SNAIL
SWIM
WATER

Made in the USA
Middletown, DE
07 November 2021